Where Is S

Story by
Sally Cowan

Illustrations by
Anne Spudvilas

"Mom! Mom!" shouted Rosa.

"Come and see Socks."

"Sh … ! Sh … ! Sh … !"
said Dad.

"**Look** at Socks!" said Rosa.

"He is running away."

Dad ran into the garden
to look for Socks.

Mom and Rosa went
into the garden, too.

"Where are you, Socks?"

said Rosa.

"Come here, Socks.

Come here to me."

Mom looked for Socks

in the leaves.

"He is not here," said Mom.

Dad looked for Socks
up in the tree.

"He is not up here,"
said Dad.

"Socks is not in the garden," said Mom.

"No," said Dad.

"Sh … ! Sh … ! Sh … !" said Rosa. "Come and look in here."

"Socks is asleep

on my bed,"

said Rosa.